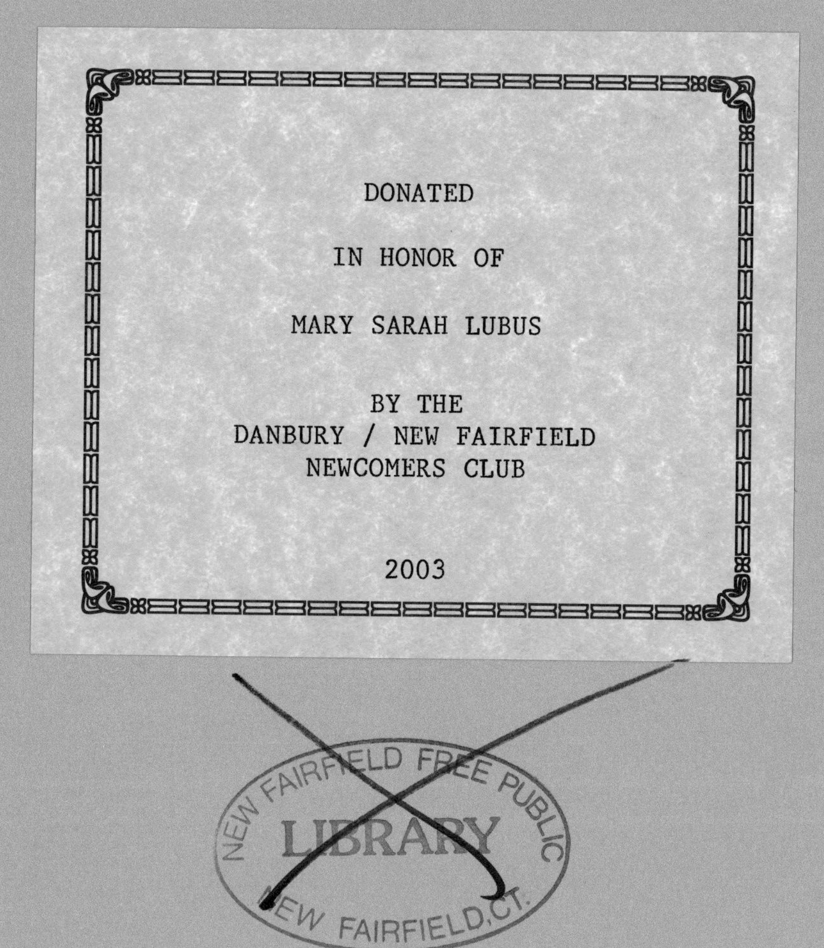
DONATED
IN HONOR OF
MARY SARAH LUBUS
BY THE
DANBURY / NEW FAIRFIELD
NEWCOMERS CLUB
2003
NEW FAIRFIELD FREE PUBLIC
LIBRARY
NEW FAIRFIELD, CT.

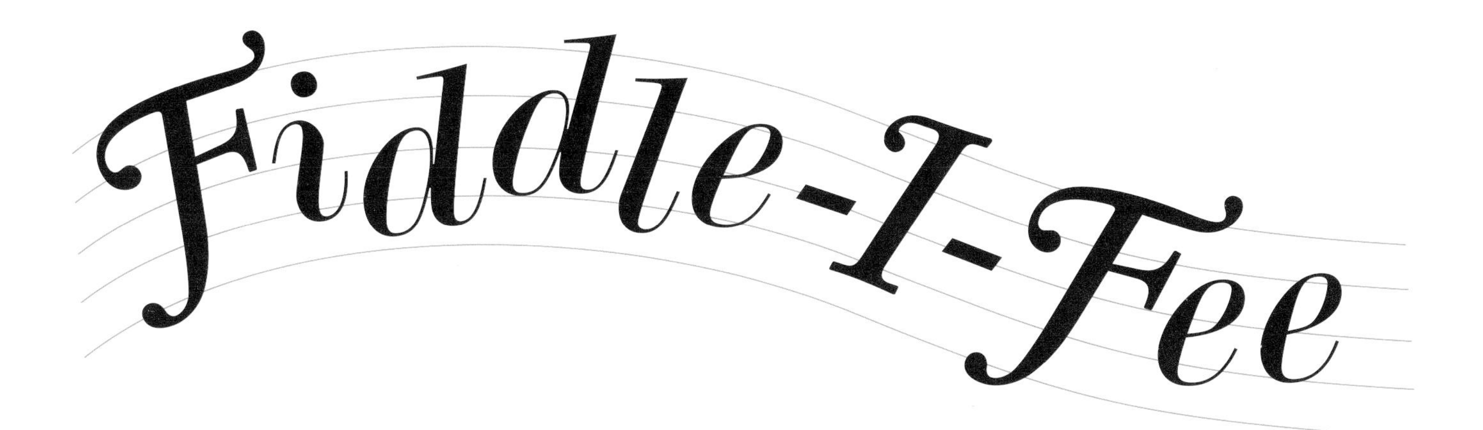


Will Hillenbrand

GULLIVER BOOKS
HARCOURT, INC.
*San Diego  New York  London*

For Naomi



www.harcourt.com

*Gulliver Books* is a trademark of Harcourt, Inc., registered in the United States of America and/or other jurisdictions.

Library of Congress Cataloging-in-Publication Data
Hillenbrand, Will.
Fiddle-i-fee/Will Hillenbrand.
p. cm.
"Gulliver Books."
Summary: In this cumulative nursery rhyme, a farmer and his wife prepare for a new baby as their animals secretly meet at night to plan a surprise of their own.
1. Folk songs, English—United States—Texts.
2. Children's songs—Texts. 3. Nursery rhymes, American.
4. Children's poetry, American. [1. Domestic animals—Songs and music. 2. Folk songs—United States.
3. Nursery rhymes.]
I. Title.
PZ8.3.H553Fi 2002
782.421642'13'0083—dc21 2001001382
ISBN 0-15-201945-6

First edition
H G F E D C B A

Printed in Singapore

The illustrations in this book were created in mixed media on vellum, painted on both sides.
The display type was set in Monotype Modern.
The text type was set in Veljovic.
Color separations by Bright Arts Ltd., Hong Kong
Printed and bound by Tien Wah Press, Singapore
This book was printed on totally chlorine-free Nymolla Art paper.
Production supervision by Sandra Grebenar and Ginger Boyer
Designed by Ivan Holmes and Will Hillenbrand

# Fiddle-I-Fee

3. I had a goose and my goose pleased me.
   I fed my goose under yonder tree.
   Goose plays hum summ, hum summ.
   Duck plays quaa quaa, quaa quaa.
   Cat plays fiddle-i-fee.

4. I had a hen and my hen pleased me.
   I fed my hen under yonder tree.
   Hen plays cimmy-chuck, cimmy-chuck, *etc.*

5. I had a pig and my pig pleased me.
   I fed my pig under yonder tree.
   Pig plays griffy, griffy, *etc.*

6. I had a cow and my cow pleased me.
   I fed my cow under yonder tree.
   Cow plays strum strum, strum strum, *etc.*

7. I had a horse and my horse pleased me.
   I fed my horse under yonder tree.
   Horse plays dub-ub, dub-ub, *etc.*

8. I had a dog and my dog pleased me.
   I fed my dog under yonder tree.
   Dog plays clickity-clack, clickity-clack, *etc.*

9. I had a sheep and my sheep pleased me.
   I fed my sheep under yonder tree.
   Sheep plays shake shake, shake shake, *etc.*

10. I had a baby and my baby pleased me.
    We fed our baby under yonder tree.
    Baby goes tee-hee, tee-hee, *etc.*

I had a cat.
My cat pleased me.
I fed my cat under yonder tree.

My cat plays fiddle-i-fee.

I had a duck.
My duck pleased me.
I fed my duck under yonder tree.

SEPTEMBER

My duck plays quaa quaa.

fiddle-i-fee

Honk
Honk
Honk

I had a goose.
My goose pleased me.
I fed my goose under yonder tree.

My goose plays hum summ.

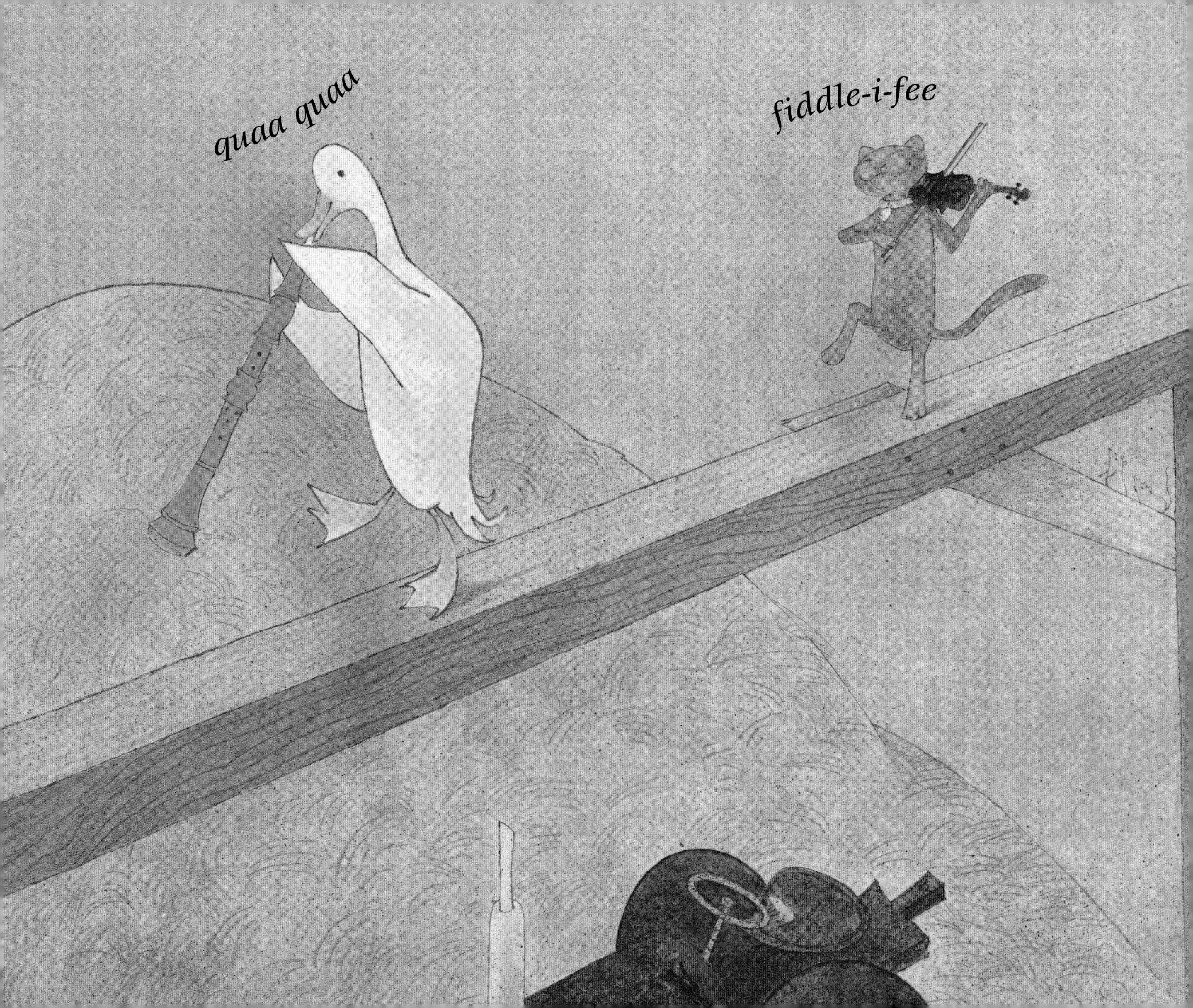
quaa quaa
fiddle-i-fee

I had a hen.
My hen pleased me.
I fed my hen under yonder tree.

Cluck
Cluck
Cluck

*My hen plays cimmy-chuck, cimmy-chuck.*

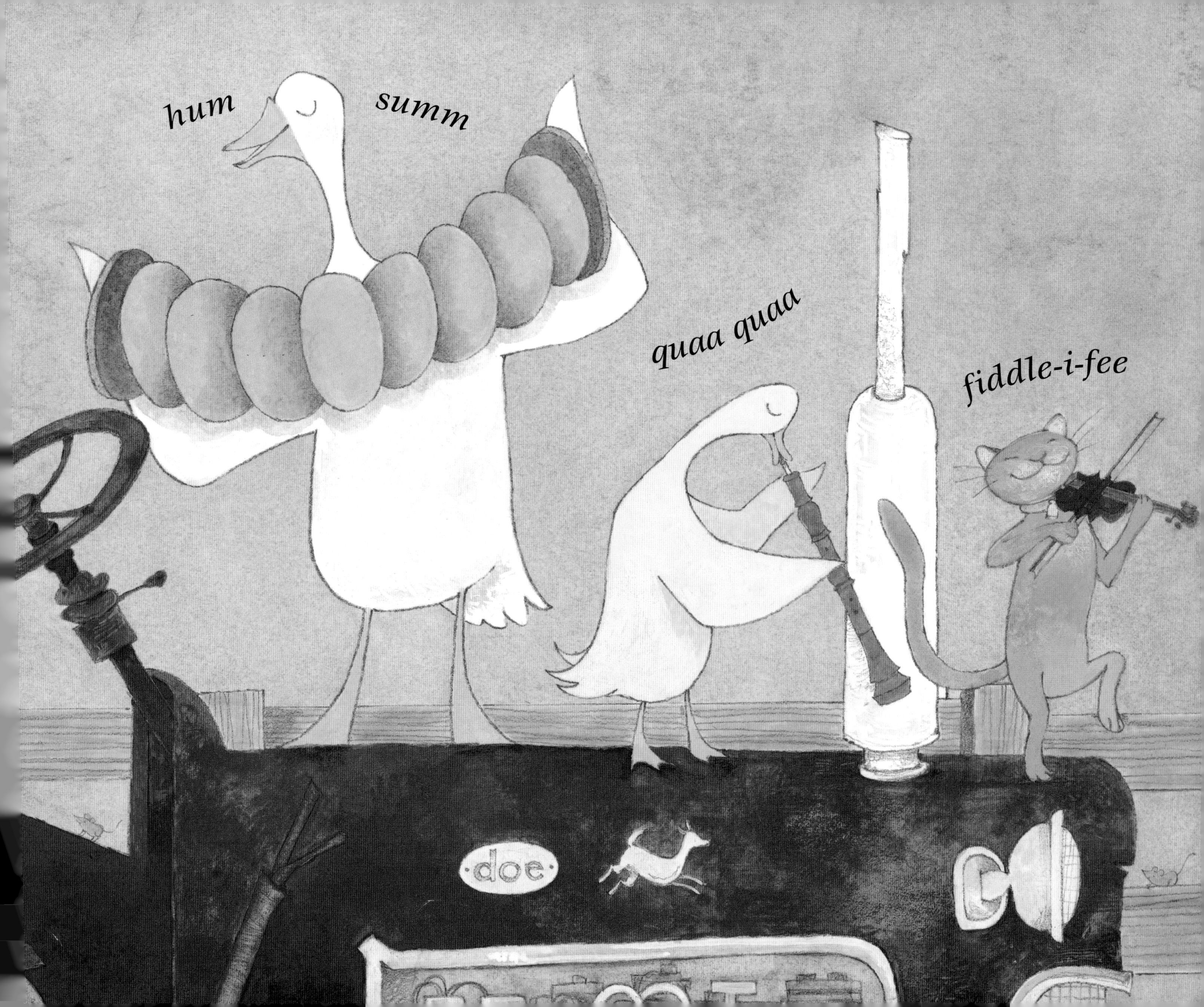
hum
summ
quaa quaa
fiddle-i-fee
doe

I had a pig.
My pig pleased me.
I fed my pig under yonder tree.

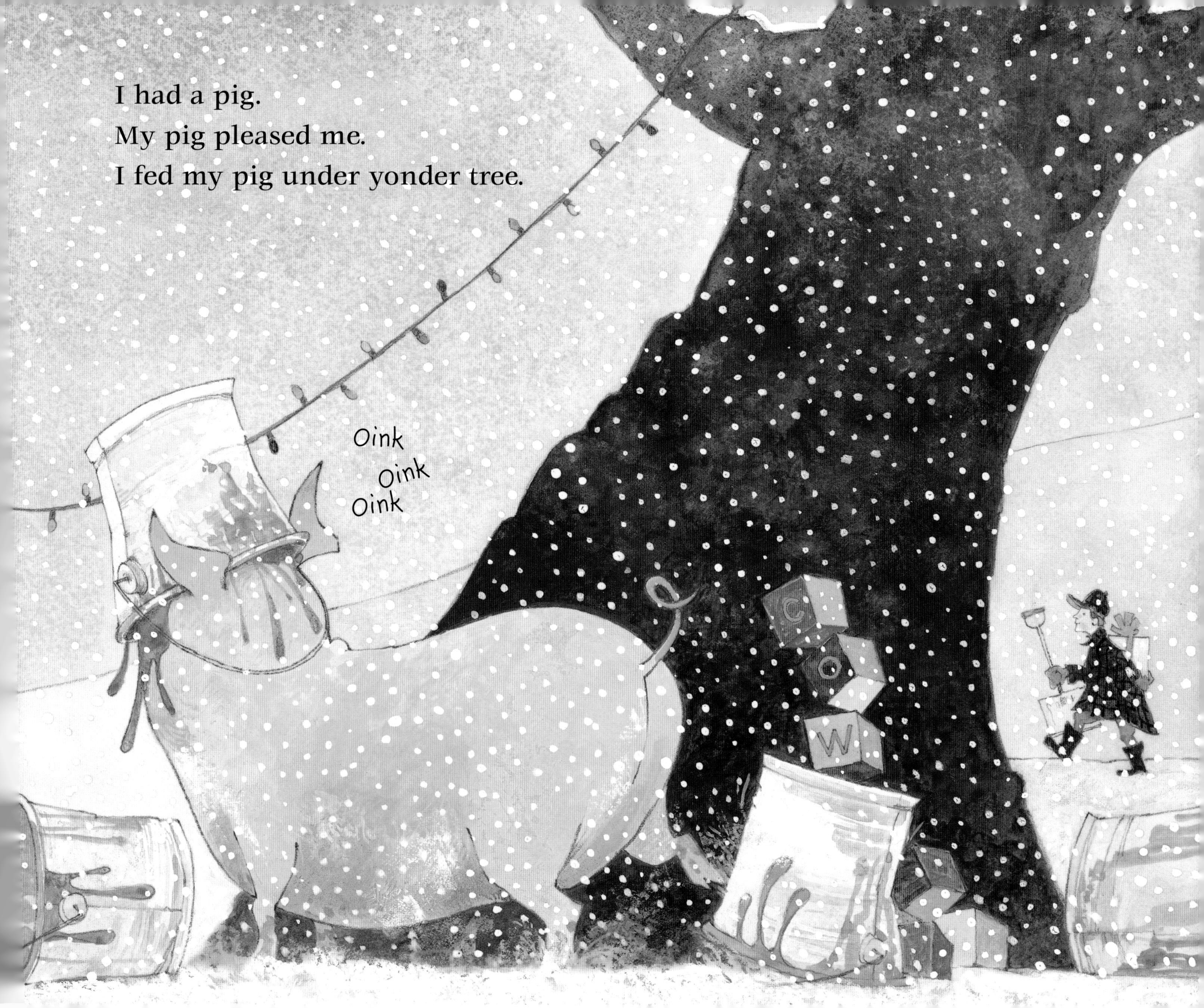

Oink
Oink
Oink

My pig plays griffy, griffy.
cimmy-chuck, cimmy-chuck

hum summ
quaa quaa
fiddle-i-fee
doe

I had a cow.
My cow pleased me.
I fed my cow under yonder tree.

My cow plays
strum
strum.
griffy,
griffy

hum
summ
quaa quaa
fiddle-i-fee
cimmy-chuck, cimmy-chuck

I had a horse.
My horse pleased me.
I fed my horse under yonder tree.

Neigh
Neigh
Neigh

My horse plays
dub-ub.
strum strum

griffy, griffy
cimmy-chuck, cimmy-chuck
quaa quaa
fiddle-i-fee
hum
summ

Bowwow
Bowwow
Bowwow

I had a dog.
My dog pleased me.
I fed my dog under yonder tree.

My dog plays clickity-clack.
dub- ub
strum strum

cimmy-chuck, cimmy-chuck
griffy, griffy
quaa quaa
fiddle-i-fee
hum
summ

I had a sheep.
My sheep pleased me.
I fed my sheep under yonder tree.

APRIL
1 2 3 4 5
6 7 8 9 10 11 12
13 14 15 16 17 18 19
20 21 22 23 24 25 26
27 28 29 30
Sweet ♥ Sweet
BABY

My sheep plays shake shake.
dub-ub
strum strum
clickity-clack

griffy, griffy
cimmy-chuck,
cimmy-chuck
hum summ
quaa quaa
fiddle-i-fee

I had a baby.
My baby pleased me.
We fed our baby under yonder tree.

NEW FAIRFIELD FREE PUBLIC
LIBRARY
NEW FAIRFIELD, CT.